MARRYING THE SCARRED SOLDIER

IRIS WEST

CHAPTER ONE

Willow

IF ANYONE HAD told me I'd willingly put myself in a relationship again, I'd have laughed my head off. But here I am, in a secluded wooden cabin in the woods, married and willing at that. Out of the corner of my eyes, I take in my husband's massive shoulders, thick legs, almost shoulder length hair and beard. He's looking at the TV so I can't see his deep-set eyes and the other side of his face, yet, I've memorized their light gray color and the pink, rough looking skin on the right side of his face. A shiver runs through me.

Ransom turns toward me. I look away. Heat creeps up my face when I'm caught staring. I look at the cracking logs in the log burner and the heat in my body intensifies. I bite my lip. For years I didn't feel any desire and thought part of me had dried up with the bitterness from my past life, but the moment I laid eyes on Ransom a few months ago, lust stirred in me.

"Do you want to watch something else?"

His voice is deep, steady and quiet, just like him. It makes me think of strength and loyalty. As if it's the voice of someone I can trust. Which is bull considering his humongous size and bad boy look. Ransom Boyd is not the type of man a mother would look at and think of as a prospective husband for her daughter. That doesn't faze me because one, I don't have a mother or father, and two, I lived with the kind of white collar, handsome boy society believed made perfect husband material and went through hell.

"No, I like this." And I do like the soap that's playing. It's just that there's zero chance of me paying attention to it tonight. "I really don't mind if you want to watch something else, too." His profile from the matchmaking agency said he likes nature shows.

"Willow."

Even though I'm already looking at him, something in his voice and face makes me more alert.

"Didn't we decide we'd take turns choosing?" He asks.

I nod.

"It'll be my turn tomorrow. If I change the channel, you'll have two nights of watching animals in the wild. I won't let go of the remote."

His lip lifts a fraction. Is that an attempt at a joke? My own lips tug up.

"I'll keep the drama on." I lift the remote off the coffee table and put it on the armrest on my side of the couch. Then I pick it up and press pause. "Ask away if there's anything you want explained." I've watched a third of the show but I started it at the beginning so he won't feel lost.

Ransom scratches his beard. "Why did Michael say he committed the crime when he clearly didn't?"

I can't help the smile that tugs at my lips. "You'll see."

Suddenly, some of the tension in me disappears. He's watching. It may seem like a small thing, but to me, it's a step in the right direction for this marriage that's based on the small amount of information we exchanged about each other on the matchmaking agency profile and the couple of times we met. He's trying to get along with me.

The first time I saw Ransom was three months ago, which was about nine months after I arrived in Blossom Ford on the run from my partner of four years. I was shocked by the lust he stirred in me, but I didn't approach him. I was too busy surviving. Stopping myself thinking about him at night became a problem I couldn't solve, so I stopped trying and when I felt horny, it was his eyes and body I saw when I made myself come.

Six weeks ago, my high school friend Coleen called and said my ex-partner was looking for me again. For days, I was paralyzed with fear. My ex-partner had found me before when I run to Chicago. I'd thought being in a large city would make it almost impossible for him to find me, but I was wrong and barely escaped. I ran as far south as I could go until my money run out in Blossom Ford.

I made a home for me and my little boy, Jordan. Jordan loves the friends he has made at Smart Teddies Day care, and I love my job there. I don't want to leave Blossom ford.

As I watched Jordan play on the swings at the park one Sunday, thinking about what to do, I sensed someone beside me. Terrified, I'd looked sideways to see Granny Tallulah sit on the other side of the bench I was sitting on. I'd seen her wandering about town when I first arrived in Blossom Ford a few weeks later I learned she had dementia so everyone in town looked out for her and walked her home if they found her out late at night or wandering the streets without shoes or a coat.

I think she thought I was her daughter because she always wanted to know what my little boy was eating and how he was doing and gave me advice to make him "big and strong" as she often said. That day, as I was leaving the park, Granny Tallulah grabbed my arm and said the strangest words. Her daughter would find me a husband who would protect me and my little boy. I remember the shiver that runs up my spine. Not even Angel knew about my past.

As I headed home, I told myself Granny Tallulah

was probably speaking generally, but the thought that the agency had matched a lot of happy couples in Blossom Ford, including my newlywed friend Angel and her husband, kept intruding into my mind. I signed up and when I was matched with Ransom; I recognized him straight away. The fact he was ex-military and lived in the mountains grabbed my attention and wouldn't let go. I started wondering if maybe he could protect us. That it'd be harder to be found in the mountains.

His profile said he was looking for companionship and love. I should have skipped past his picture because I wasn't looking for love. My ex-partner was my high school sweetheart. When I fell for and started living with him, I thought I'd at last found true happiness. Instead, I'd swapped the hell of bad foster care and a rough group home for the hell of an abusive partner.

I hadn't planned to mention anything when I met Ransom. The fear he'd change his mind about our arranged marriage after learning about my past was absolute. However, despite his rough looks, or maybe because of it, I'd sensed an honesty in Ransom that made me ashamed of lying to him. Suddenly, hiding my past didn't feel right, and I told him I was running from my ex.

"I spent almost all of my adult life protecting people. It's the one thing I'm good at," he'd said in that steady voice of his and although a part of me was terrified of trusting a man with my life, I didn't have many other choices and went ahead with the marriage.

Seeing him try to keep to the small arrangement we made about taking turns doing what we each like together gives me some hope of us getting along.

CHAPTER TWO

Ransom

I'M NOT THE type of man to regret a decision I made, but a tiny part of me wonders if Willow would be better with a man who could give her the type of life she deserves. A beautiful woman like her shouldn't be with a scarred, reclusive man whose only company is books and animals. Problem is I've never been a gentleman. Now that Willow has decided to be my wife, I'm going to do everything in my power to make sure she never wants to leave.

Sitting on the sofa with her in my small living room feels good. Even though we're both nervous.

I've tried to make her as comfortable as possible, but I can tell she's not really watching the drama. And I don't blame her. What woman would feel comfortable on her first wedding night with a husband she's only met twice and doesn't know how to sweet talk her?

"Another beer?" As soon as the drama is over, I ask. I'm not trying to get her drunk; I just want her to relax a little.

Willow nods.

I pad to the kitchen area and grab us a couple of chilled bottles. My eyes run over every part of the small cabin. Checking everything is fine is a habit I can't get rid of, even though I retired from the military three years ago. Now that Willow and Jordan are here, there's a heightened sense of responsibility within me. Instead of feeling burdened by it, I welcome it. It makes me feel like I'm part of something important. Like my life has purpose again.

Willow is checking out the only picture with people in the room when I return to the sitting area. She leans over to see it better, and I drag my eyes away from her curvy ass just before she turns around. I place the beers on the table and watch her walk over. She looks striking in an ivory knitted dress that reaches all the way to her feet. The soft wool molds her rounded breasts and thighs and is a beautiful contrast to the silky, black waves of hair bouncing past her shoulders.

"That's a lovely family picture? Is that your brother? Was he in the military with you? You and your sisters look so young."

I down half of my bottle. I'm not used to talking about my life like this, but it's natural that Willow has questions about me. In order to give this marriage a good go, I'm going to have to open up about some things in my life.

"That was taken about ten years ago. I must have been around thirty-one. That is Danny. He was the Walters' only son. We were more like brothers of the heart. That's what he used to say anyway, after he brought me here to meet his family. He died in Afghanistan during a military operation." I trail my fingers across the side of the bottle and watch the moisture there as it drips onto my jeans.

"I'm sorry. I didn't mean to bring up terrible memories."

There's compassion in Willow's eyes.

"It's been a while." But I missed him every day. I missed the loss of his dreams. Danny was only a few months away from leaving the military. He'd dreamed of running a small farm back home in Blossom Ford with a girl and a bunch of kids.

"It looks like you cared for him a lot. You were all so loving at the registry office that even though you were the only dark-haired and eyed person in the family, I thought you were blood related."

"Danny's sisters and parents are like that. The day that photo was taken was the first time I ever felt like I was part of a family. It was also my first time visiting the Walters and Blossom Ford. I came another two times with Danny and fell in love with these mountains. I joined the army straight out of high school. When I retired three years ago, I settled here."

Somehow, doing some things my friend had wanted to do felt like Danny was doing them. It was a small way to give back to Danny the friendship he'd shared with me.

That's why when Mary-Jayne, Danny's youngest sister, told me I had thirty minutes to meet the bride I knew nothing about, I didn't kill her. She registered me at the matchmaking agency and responded to Willow's queries, all without my knowledge.

She looked so much like Danny when she explained I'd never have accepted to register for the agency and the reason she'd given me brief notice was because she knew that even though I didn't consider myself a gentleman; I wasn't callous enough to stand up a young woman who believed she'd met her perfect husband without an explanation.

Although I'd been mad with her, the pleading look in her blue eyes, so much like Danny's when I found out he'd sent my amateur photos to a nature magazine without my consent, eased my anger.

It also helped that the moment I saw Willow's curvy figure and the haunted look in her coffee brown eyes, I knew I'd go ahead with the arranged marriage.

Willow stares at me like she wants to ask something, but shakes her head. She takes a long sip of her beer. "I know what it's like to have a family of the heart. My friend Angel and my co-workers at Day care are like that. Especially Angel. She's like a sister, or what I imagine a sister would be like. Her granny, you saw her at the registry office, treats Jordan as if he were her great grandkid. It's the first time Jordan and I have felt welcomed as part of a family."

She blinks and turns away, but isn't fast enough for my trained eyes. I spotted tears in her eyes before she blinked.

"Mr. Clark threatened to kill me if I mistreated you."

"What? Angel's dad?"

I nod. It's not something I ever intended telling her, but those tears got me thinking she might find comfort from hearing this.

"What did he say?" The tears are back, but funnily enough, she's smiling too.

"He got close and looked me straight in the eyes." I've never been good at acting, but I change my voice. "Son, you look like someone who can use his fists and a gun, but if you hurt Willow, I'll find a way to kill you."

Willow giggles.

I don't know if she's laughing at my weird acting, but I feel myself smile. Her coffee brown eyes are full of mirth and her even white teeth shine against the nude gloss on her lips. She crosses both her legs under her and faces me fully.

"He must have looked a sight. I'm so sorry."

"You don't look it."

She claps a hand over her mouth as if to hide her laughter.

"I was touched, actually. It's the first time anyone ever said those words to me. It made me feel like part of a family, too."

"Thank you for telling me."

I'm wondering if she spotted the red in my cheeks.

She also plays with the condensation on her beer bottle. "I had a couple of foster parents, but mostly I grew up in group homes. I didn't click anywhere, so don't really have a family. It's nice to know Angel's dad watched out for me like that."

All she told me about Jordan's father was that he was abusive and she was running from him. I don't think she's ready to talk about that, so I don't ask, but I know very well what it's like to be part of a family with an abusive member.

"Would you like another beer?"

She covers a yawn. "Sorry. I'm exhausted. I don't know why, it's not like there was lots to organize for the wedding. All we did was book a table at Jackson's Diner for our families."

But that wasn't all. Apart from moving their small amount of baggage, Willow had to deal with canceling her tenancy, stopping her bills and moving in with a man she hardly knew. Considering she was running away from a man she'd once trusted; it must have taken a great deal of courage to trust another man with protecting her.

After the abuse I suffered at my father's hands and my mother's abandonment, it took me years to let

Danny in and build a friendship with him. Although it wasn't the same, I was good friends with the other men I served with, so I suppose having to learn to trust the other men in my team with my safety helped me open up a little.

"Sleep with Jordan tonight."

"Are you sure?"

"We agreed to take things slow and get to know each other." I'm crazy with wanting Willow, but I don't want her sleeping with me because she's grateful. Also, although she doesn't seem bothered by my scar — apart from the initial surprise when we first met — I'm not crazy enough to scare her away by showing her the rest of my body. My burn scar runs the entire length of my right side.

Tonight, my cock will have to settle for my fist.

CHAPTER THREE

Willow

I THOUGHT I'D have a hard time sleeping. Before I arrived in Blossom Ford, I'd never lived in a small town. I had trouble falling asleep the first couple of days. Apart from the sound of a few animals, it's even quieter here in the woods. Add to that the fact that Ransom was sleeping in the room next door, it all made the cabin not conducive to sleeping. I remember nothing after my head hit the pillow, though, so I must have dozed off straight away. The daylight in the room wakes me up.

I remove Jordan's arm from my chest and place it against his small body. He's only five, but tries to be grown up when he's awake. His father is a selfish prick and I'm a bag of insecurities behind my tough exterior, so I don't know how he became such a wise and gentle little boy.

I kiss the honey-gold of his soft cheek; glad he could get a good night's sleep and quietly leave the bed. It's half past seven, way past my usual wake up time for work. I took a few days off day care so Jordan and I can get to know Ransom and our new home. I remember the humble expression on his face when he said he had enough money coming in from his pension and photography work for a decent living for the three of us so I could stop work if I wanted. It touched me. But the fact I didn't work was one way Luke used to insult me, even though he was the main reason I couldn't work—he'd hated me going out.

Ransom's not in the kitchen. When I enter the bathroom, the shower is damp and there is a faint citrusy scent in the air. An image of Ransom showering enters my mind, making my core clench. I blow out air and switch on the tap. This wasn't the time to think about my hot husband. Quickly, I wash and dress for the day in the bedroom, still careful not to wake Jordan, then head to the kitchen.

I open the refrigerator. It's bursting with groceries. There's a popular brand of kids' yoghurt I'm almost positive Ransom got for Jordan. I pull out eggs and bacon.

The front door opens, letting in a light breeze.

"Morning." Ransom walks in. His light brown hair is dark with damp.

The shower scene pops into my mind. I duck my

head and greet the eggs. I just don't know what's gotten into me since the day I first saw Ransom. It's like my body was making up for the years it didn't get any action.

Ransom takes out two frying pans and puts them on the cooker. "I'll make some pancakes while you fry the eggs and bacon."

"I can do it all. It won't take long."

Ransom pauses in the act of opening a bag of flour. "I've never cooked with a woman before. It's one of my fantasies."

I blink. It's such an innocent fantasy. Why am I blushing? But even as the question forms in my mind, I know the answer. It's his deep voice and the way he looks at me. Steady, like he's eying me up before he takes me. I shiver.

"Are you cold?"

I shake my head. I dated Luke in high school and started living with him when we graduated and I found out I was pregnant. He's the only man I've known, and he'd stopped finding me attractive as soon as I started showing. I have little experience with men, but I'm almost sure I've interpreted the look in Ransom's clear gray eyes correctly.

His movements are sure as he breaks eggs and whips batter. His hands are large, like everything about him. I first noticed the burn mark on his right hand at the registry office when he put a ring on my finger. For the first time, I realize he always has his unburned side to me. Is he conscious about his scar? And does it go all the way down his body? It's too early in our relationship to ask. I understand all too well how sometimes we want to keep things to ourselves.

"How is the fantasy so far? Is it close to what you hoped for?" I tease.

"It's close. I'm enjoying it."

I toy with the desire to ask what would make it complete, as he places a perfectly browned pancake on a plate. "What's missing?"

"A back hug. That always happens in the scenes I've seen."

I stare at him. He's watching me with that intense look in his eyes again. The sizzling of oil draws my attention from him.

"I've seen that too. I've always wondered what it'd feel like. Maybe we could try it one day." I can't believe the playful voice is coming from my throat.

"I'd like that."

"How do you like your eggs?"

By the time we finish cooking, I know how Ransom likes his breakfast and what his favorite food is. And he knows mine too.

The knowledge brings about a strange feeling in me. It's been a long time since a man has shown interest in me.

"Mommy," a bleary-eyed Jordan calls out.

I place the plate I'm holding on the table and hug my little boy.

"Morning Jordan," Ransom says from the stove.

Jordan watches him for a while before he answers. My heart goes out to him. It took me a while to figure out that not answering people immediately was one way Jordan tests people. His dad lashed out if he didn't answer straight away.

Jordan's eyes go to the birdcage in one corner of the room. There's a tiny sparrow there.

"His name is Muller. He hurt one of his wings. We'll release him once he's better. Would you like to feed him?" Ransom asks.

Jordan nods.

"Get dressed. I'll show you how after breakfast."

Warmth fills my heart and I throw Ransom a look of gratitude.

CHAPTER FOUR

Ransom

"YOU WEREN'T KIDDING when you said it was colder up here," Willow says as we head away from the cabin.

Even though it's the beginning of spring and down the mountain, it's already noticeably warmer, it's still cold up here. Willow looks cute in one of my woolen hats.

"Are you warm enough?" I ask.

She points to the thick scarf around her head, which Danny's mom knitted for me. She faces the sky with widespread arms and closes her eyes.

"It feels great to be out here. I can smell the fresh, crispy air."

"It's one thing I love about living here."

I watch Jordan as he chases a squirrel until it

disappears into the thick branches of a tree.

"I'd always thought of myself as a city girl, but I can see myself living here. Especially since you have electricity and running water."

I chuckle. It sounds strange to my ears. After Danny left, it was hard for my teammates and me to laugh. When I suffered burns during another explosion on the day I finished my service and was due to fly home, it became even harder.

"You have a delightful laugh. You should do it more often."

I can feel myself blushing. Fuck it, I'm like a teenager on his first date. It's Willow. Yesterday, she made me smile. Today, she's making me laugh.

To hide my embarrassment, I march over to Jordan, who's still staring up at the tree. I peer up and my breath catches. The squirrel is looking down at us. He looks magnificent, with the branches stretching high above him.

Quietly, so I don't scare it away, I reach for my camera. I capture the scenery before the little animal bolts.

"Can I see?" Jordan asks.

I squat. We both look at the image on the screen.

"Its eyes are huge," Jordan says, awe in his voice.

"It's a beautiful picture!" Willow exclaims beside us.

I nod.

"Will you submit it to a magazine? How much do you get for a photo like this?" she asks.

I shrug. "Depends. Anything from a couple of hundred to a couple of thousand bucks, depending on who's buying."

"Isn't it a cool job Mommy? Can I do it when I grow up? I'd get to take photos of animals and plants all day!"

I chuckle. "It's an awesome job."

We walk for about an hour and stop a few times to take pictures of animals and interesting plants, and for me to point out the nearest house, which is about half an hour away from ours. Calling the cabin ours feels strange but good. Willow and Jordan have been here for less than twenty-four hours and already, I'm feeling like we're a family.

We spend the day playing games and watching kids' programs on TV until it's Jordan's bedtime.

"Mom, can Uncle Ransom read my bedtime story?"

I led teams of men and carried out complex operations during my military service, but the fear I feel that I'll disappoint Jordan is something I've never experienced.

When he falls asleep after only a few sentences, I glance at Willow. "Is he supposed to fall asleep this quickly? I tried to change the tone of my voice to make the story more interesting, but maybe I made it sound boring."

"You were perfect," she whispers. "He's usually asleep by this time. The walk must have tired him out as well."

We watch a documentary on the geographical channel. Despite what I said yesterday, I offer to let her watch the drama we started yesterday.

"It's your turn with the remote, remember?"

Once again, being so close to Willow makes it hard to focus. I can smell the shower gel and perfume she used. I don't even know what it is exactly, but the scent of is driving me wild.

When she says goodnight, I'm not sure whether to be relieved or happy. But then she leans across me and kisses my cheek. It's an innocent peck, but my whole body goes on alert. I stare at Willow's soft lips.

Her tongue darts out of her mouth, and she licks those luscious lips. Even though I promised myself I'd take things slow with her, I can't stop myself from rubbing my thumb across her wet lip. A couple of beats pass, then she sucks my thumb.

Groaning, I snake my hand across her nape and pull her towards me. An inch away from her parted lips, I pause. When she doesn't pull away, I kiss her. Deeply, like a man who's been starved of water for too long. She kisses me back, her tongue dueling with mine as if she's just as ravenous as I am.

I angle her head for a deeper kiss. My hands rove over the swell of her breasts. She moans and my sanity returns.

I put my head against hers. "We're supposed to be taking this slow. Are you okay?"

"Yes," she whispers against my mouth.

My cock hardens. I pull away. "Goodnight Willow."
I scoot as far away as I can to avoid touching her again.

CHAPTER FIVE

Willow

IT'S BEEN TWO weeks since I married Ransom. I've been back at work for a week and today, I'm working in the baby room. I change a nappy, crooning to the little girl. This is the best part of childhood. I could spend the whole day with the babies in here and still be smiling at the end of my shift.

I hope Ransom wants children because I'd like Jordan to have brothers and sisters. Thinking about babies makes me think about kissing Ransom.

We've kissed every single night since that first time. But that's all we've done. I'm so frustrated, I spend every free moment thinking about whether to tell Ransom it's time to move to the next base or, better still, the last base.

But what if my body repulses him? Luke used to say looking at me made him lose his erection. What if Ransom feels the same way?

I've never been dainty. I've always been big boned. Being five feet eight didn't help. Boys had never really wanted to talk to me. So, when the best-looking boy at school showed interest, I was overjoyed. I was okay with my body, but the foster system had thrown me a few curve balls, so my self-esteem wasn't exactly high. I fell for Luke's easy charm and looks. Believing he loved me, I gave myself to him.

Soon after graduation, I started showing and putting on weight. That's when I noticed Luke change. He became verbally and physically abusive. My body became a turn off. After Jordan was born, I tried everything to lose weight, but nothing helped. Luke didn't want me anymore, but he wouldn't let me leave either. As his behavior worsened, so did my self-confidence.

Being away from him helped. So did having friends like Angel, who was curvy too and loved her body. I desperately want to be with Ransom, but it isn't easy to get rid of the worry he might not like my body.

Every weekday, he drives Jordan and me to daycare and picks us up. There's no bus that goes up the mountain, so I'm grateful he's happy to drive us. We spend our evenings in front of the fire, watching TV, reading or playing games.

The door to the nursery opens. Angel sticks her head

round.

I rush over and hug her. "It's so nice to see you. Are you popping in to visit?"

"Yes. Oh, I've missed this room."

I chuckle. "Really? Have you been sending Liv and Ollie to your mom's?"

Angel laughs too. "I don't have to. Mom and Grannie turn up all the time. They spoil the twins so much, those adorable brats are quite happy to go off with their grandparents and great gran whenever they get the chance. But how are you?"

Angel stands in front of me and I feel like I'm on display for her. "Stop that already. I'm fine."

Angel shakes her head. "We haven't really talked about your wedding. I knew you met someone. You've had that look of someone who's in love for a while now."

"Love? Just because you and Liam are head over heels with each other, you're seeing the l word everywhere, right?."

Angel pats a baby that's stirring. She lowers her voice. "You deserve to be happy. I think you and Ransom will make a lovely couple. So, how are things really going?"

"We're taking it easy."

"Yeah? And how is that going?"

"He's kind and wonderful with Jordan. I feel like I've won the lottery."

"Why were you frowning, then?"

"I was?"

"What's the matter?"

Would Angel understand? "I'm worried Ransom might not like me."

Angel looks blank.

"All of me." I point at my body.

"Willow, some men like curvy women. Actually, a lot of the men in Blossom Ford. I don't think he would have married you if he weren't attracted to you. Besides, the way he looked at you during your wedding, he's into you."

As Angel says goodbye, I fervently hope Angel is right. Because I really like Ransom and want to spend the rest of my life with him. I like the way he cares for me and Jordan and his fairness and honesty. I like our quiet life and have fallen completely in love with his wooden cabin and the woods surrounding it. It feels like home.

I'm not the type to hold things in for long. After losing my fighting spirit when I was with Luke, I let him hurt me until he hit Jordan and I woke up from the nightmare I'd been living in. I'd tried to get away from him before without success, but seeing my son hurt gave me the determination I needed to finally run from him successfully.

I'm done with not speaking up for myself. Tonight, I'll let Ransom know I'm ready to go all the way with him. What happens next will be up to him.

CHAPTER SIX

Ransom

THERE'S SOMETHING DIFFERENT about Willow. I notice it the moment I set eyes on her. I open the door for Jordan and make sure his seatbelt is tucked in properly.

"Is everything alright?" I ask as I drive up the mountain.

She tells me about Angel's visit and Jordan pipes in about his day, but I still can't work out what's wrong.

The moment I park the car in front of the cabin, I know there's an intruder inside. The door isn't properly shut. Near the steps, there's a dent against the wall, like someone swung a bat at it.

"Wait Jordan," I stop the little boy as he's about to open the door. I turn to Willow. "Stay in the car. Call the cops, there's someone in the house," I whisper to her.

Her eyes widen. She frantically searches the cabin, then looks at Jordan.

I switch off the headlights.

"Don't leave the car."

"Where are you going? Shouldn't we head back to town?"

"Willow, trust me. It'll be fine. Sit in the back with Jordan and call the cops. Remember, I'm good at protecting people?"

She nods and scrambles to the back as I leave the car.

I lean casually against the door of the truck and check the CCTV app on my phone. There are three men. I fast forward to see if any of them came out, but they all remained inside.

They're armed with baseball bats. I slide my cell phone into my back pocket and fish out my keys, whistling.

The porch lights switch on as I climb the stairs. I insert my key into the keyhole and pretend to be surprised when the door swings back. I remove my phone and turn on the flashlight. As soon as I enter the cabin, a bat swings at me. Easily, I avoid it. I don't take any chances and quickly neutralize the untrained men inside, striking in the right places to make them unconscious. I switch on the light, then get rope from a cupboard in the kitchen area and tie them up, making sure the knots are tight.

"I'm okay. I tied the intruders up, but it's best if I'm

here. Stay in the car until the cops arrive," I tell Willow over the phone.

"Is it Luke?"

One man is identical to the photo Willow showed me of Jordan's father. "Yes."

A sigh. "Be careful."

I hang up the phone as Luke spews a string of curses. "Son of a bitch. Untie me. Do you know who my father is?"

"He's running for mayor. Has a pretty good chance of winning."

Apprehension enters Luke's eyes.

"I have a few contacts of my own. I can ensure the CCTV footage of you and your friends damaging, breaking and entering my property gets released to the opposition and the press. How would your father feel about that?"

"You're bullshitting. Do you think I'm stupid? I looked around before I came in. There were no cameras."

I press play on my cell and turn the screen to Luke. One of his friends wakes up and starts crying when he sees himself on my cell. The footage is of the best quality. The faces are clearly visible.

I stop the video.

"I recorded our conversation as well," I add. Sirens sound in the distance.

Luke and the conscious man contort themselves, trying to break free of the ropes.

"If you ever come crawling back here, you'll regret it. Willow's no longer alone. You won't be able to hurt her anymore. Keep your mouth shut as you leave." I say in my coldest voice. I don't feel any remorse as Luke soils his pants. Bullies like him pretend to be strong until they meet someone they can't handle.

I give a concise statement to the cops and step outside before the officers are ready to leave. I don't want Jordan to see his father, especially in the state he's in.

The little boy is crying when I open the door. Willow is trying to comfort him. She's holding back tears, but I can see she won't last much longer.

"Look at him," I whisper into Willow's ear. "He won't ever hurt you again."

She looks out of the window and her mouth falls open. Luke's no longer trussed up like a chicken but is in handcuffs, yet there's no disguising his soiled trousers and the beaten air about him. I hope seeing him like that will help lessen the fear Willow has of Luke.

"Did he soil himself?" She whispers back.

I nod.

She blinks back tears. Admiration replaces the fear. "What did you do to him?"

"I threatened him with CCTV footage of him entering and breaking. His father is running for mayor. He'd love to have that scandal about his son ruin his campaign."

"He's always feared his father. That's one reason he didn't marry me. They didn't approve of me."

"It's their loss, Willow."

She nods.

"Mommy? Is daddy here?"

My heart constricts. How could a father terrify his little boy like this? Is that what I looked like when I was Jordan's age? Jordan has a fierce mom protecting him. By the time I turned five, my mom had fled.

"Jordan, it was a bear," I say and ruffle his hair.

His eyes round, just like Willow's. "Look at me. I'm okay. I took care of the bear and saved your mom and you."

He sniffles.

"For a long time, my job was protecting people. Your dad will never hurt you or your mom again. Because I'm here to make sure you're both safe. Okay?"

He nods.

"Stay here a little longer. I'm going to clean the house."

CHAPTER SEVEN

Willow

WE FINALLY GOT Jordan to sleep. In the sitting room, I wrap my arms around Ransom and listen to the crackling of the fire. His arms tighten around me and I finally feel safe.

"You ate little. Do you want a snack?"

I shake my head. Now, more than before, I want no more uncertainties between us. "I've been thinking about something the past few days."

"What is it?"

"I'm ready to go all the way. If you'll have me, I want to be your true wife. How do you feel about it?"

He coughs. Clears his throat.

"Are you saying that because of what happened tonight? I don't want you to give yourself to me out of gratitude."

I shift around on the sofa until I'm straddling him and touching both of his cheeks, the scarred and the good. "I'm falling in love with you. The fact you can protect me and Jordan is part of the reason. But it's not the only reason. I've been feeling like this for the past few days. I love the way you make me feel like a queen. The way you care for the injured animals in the woods warms me up. I'm falling for you because you're you, Ransom."

I frown. "Actually, I fell in lust with you the first time I saw you in town, a little while before I joined the matchmaking agency. I'd think of you when I touched myself."

He blinks twice, then picks me up and deposits me on the bed in his bedroom. He goes to the wall, switches on the light and then comes and stands by the bed. Slowly, he undresses until he's standing naked before me.

I get up and touch the burned skin down the right side of his torso and hip. It's darker and rougher than the left-hand side of his body. I put my lips where my hands touch and kiss down his chest, on both sides. I can feel my panties getting wet.

I touch his cock. He's large there as well. I lick my lips, wondering if he'd fit inside my mouth. I kneel in front of him, but Ransom stops me with a strangled cry and hands on my shoulders.

"What's the matter?" I ask, staring at his engorged shaft as it stretches towards my lips.

When he doesn't answer, I look up. He's wiping tears. I freeze.

"Did I hurt you?"

He lifts me up. His shoulders shake and I realize he's laughing.

"I bloody love you, Willow." His lips crush down on mine. He rips my top and pulls down my pants.

I cover my tummy. Of all my bits, that's the part of me Luke hated the most. "The lights." I want to hide under the covers but am worried about my tummy being on display.

"You're stunning, Willow. Let me see all of you, like you did with me."

Gently, he pulls my hands away.

"Look at me," Ransom commands. "See how I'm dying for you?"

Sure enough, his cock is still standing proud, larger than it was.

He takes my hand and rubs it up and down his shaft.

Moisture seeps down my thigh. I'm so turned on right now.

"Make love to me, Ransom," I plead.

He pushes me on the bed and inserts a finger into me.

"God, Willow, you're ready for me. I wanted our first time to be crazy good for you. I don't think I can last long enough." His words are breathy on my nipple.

I bend my knees and guide him into me. I breathe against the burn as Ransom inches into me. He grabs my cheeks and kisses me until he's all the way in.

"Are you okay?" He rasps against my lips.

My hands are damp from the sweat on his back.

I squeeze my core. Ransom sets a fast-paced rhythm and I meet his every stroke, glad to at last be his. His lips graze my neck, biting lightly. I moan.

He slides a hand between us and rubs my clit. I come apart, my body arching under him as pleasure shoots into every corner of my body.

He shouts my name and bucks into me until he's spent.

I must have fallen asleep because when I open my eyes, I'm lying on Ransom's chest.

"We didn't wake up Jordan?"

"It's a little late to worry about that, sleepyhead." He brushes my hair away from my face. "I checked on him. He's fast asleep."

"Did I tell you I love you?"

"I'll never tire of hearing it. Poor Jordan, he's going to get so much love from me."

I chuckle. I love hearing Ransom joke.

He bites my neck. I shiver.

"You like this." His hands cup my ass and kneed it. I like that too, I realize. I wriggle until I come into contact with his semi-hard shaft.

"I like this too." I stroke up and down him. He must have cleaned us up because only the crown is wet. Pleasure fills me when I realize I'm making Ransom hard.

There's so much I like about him. Tears of happiness fill my eyes as I realize we have a lifetime to discover together what makes us both happy.

EPILOGUE

Ransom

Three years later

I'M SPEEDING, BUT there's no way I can drive slower. My heart is so fucking tight, it hurts to breathe. I park outside the emergency department of Blossom Ford General and rush inside.

"My wife was brought in a while ago," I say to the receptionist.

I follow the directions the man provides after I give Willow's name.

Willow is sleeping when I get to her side.

A doctor comes over as I take her hand.

"I'm her husband," I say. "What's wrong with her?"

"I'm Doctor Hemaway. Your wife has acute indigestion."

Willow wakes up, squeezes my hand.

"Hi Jamal," she says to the doctor when he approaches the bed.

"Willow. How are you feeling?"

Willow introduces us first. Jamal is Angel's husband's colleague and friend.

"The pain is gone." She frowns. "It was severe before. I couldn't breathe."

"That's how acute indigestion goes."

"I've never had it," Willow says. "Why now?"

The doctor looks at us, then smiles. "I guess you didn't know. Congratulations, you're pregnant."

I look at Willow. My chest is tight again, but it's a different tightness. We wanted a baby early in our marriage and hadn't been successful. I'd started thinking that maybe it would not happen.

"Pregnancy can cause indigestion. Always carry some medicine with you. It was nice seeing you." the doctor heads toward the nurses' station.

Willow's hand tightens in mine.

"Jordan is going to have a baby brother or sister," I say.

Tears stream down her face. "I wonder if that's why I've been so emotional. I've also put on some weight."

I laugh. "I'll love every part of you."

"We're in a hospital, big man."

She hasn't stopped calling me that since she discovered how much I love it.

"Alright, sweetheart."

I can't wait to have another child with Willow. After

realizing I'd be nothing like my dad, I've become more confident in taking care of Jordan. I love being his dad.

Every day, it becomes a little easier to speak about the wounds of my past and I thank God Willow came into   my   life.

The End

MARRYING THE OBSESSED CEO

CURVY BRIDES OF BLOSSOM FORD #7

Winona

"I'M GOING TO have a fantastic day! My colleagues will be wonderful people. There won't be anything I can't solve," I whisper to myself as I stroll towards my new job at Sanders Solutions, one of the fastest growing management consultancy firms in the country.

The nerves don't vanish, but visualizing a good day and repeating positive affirmations make me feel a little better. It helps that even though it's just gone seven, and it's late February, the sun is shining, and the air is pleasantly warm. Best of all, the cramps and migraine that had me bedridden yesterday are completely gone. If my period had started today, I would have had to call in sick on my first day, which would have sucked. I'm taking coming on yesterday as a good omen that this is going to be a successful day.

I need this job to be a success to prove to myself that moving back home to Blossom Ford isn't a complete failure. Otherwise, it'll be too hard to understand the fact that I couldn't stomach living away from home when I made a huge deal about living in Boston after college and graduate school, instead of bowing down to fate and doing what's expected of me, which is working for Blossom Ford matchmaking agency, like all the eldest girls of my family have done for generations.

Even though I missed home like crazy, I only left my job of one year at a large Boston firm when I found something better at home. My post at Sanders Solution is initially for a four-month maternity cover and the company is not as large as the top firm I worked for in Boston, still it comes with the possibility of permanent employment if I prove myself and as assistant to the CEO, it's a promotion with better pay and performance bonuses.

I have my own apartment, which means I'm independent. Popping home nearly every day and sleeping over at weekends doesn't count as being too reliant on my family's company, it just shows I missed them when I lived in away.

Besides, in a couple of weeks, Mom and Dad are going to visit one of my uncles who's been ill for a while. I'm learning to manage the agency so I can resolve any issues if anything urgent comes up. That's easier done at home. If I need any files, I can slip into the agency's small office, which is next to our house.

If only I could get my love life or lack of sorted, I'd be on cloud nine. Honestly, what twenty-five-year-old girl hasn't had at least one serious relationship? The type where one considers marriage or living together. The feeling that I'm the only one just won't go away. It's not that I'm not trying. The last three years I've been on countless dates, but they led nowhere. The men are too tall or short, too talkative or quiet, etc. My brain and body have come up with many excuses for why my dates weren't worth second chances.

And it's all because of one man. My one-night stand of three years ago. I don't even know his name, so I call him Lothario, but I remember his mesmerizing cerulean blue eyes and the feel of his beard and calloused hands on my feverish skin. I can't forget his chiseled face because I dream of him almost every night. Vivid dreams that leave me panting, my pussy wet, when I wake up.

I don't know what to do to forget him. I definitely can't forget how gentle he became when he realized I was a virgin and the tender way he wiped the blood off my thighs afterward.

My friends and I had flown to New York City from Boston for a weekend trip and when we hit the bar, they dared me to lose my virginity. They'd tried the dare countless times before, but I'd never given in. Yet, that night, from the moment I saw Lothario, I was powerless against the lust that surged within me.

I greet the two security men at the entrance of the building that houses my new company. Fishing out my badge, I let myself in and take the elevator to the top of the building. Sanders Solutions occupies the top two floors, with the executives being on the fifteenth floor.

I pass quiet desks and offices until I reach my room. Light peeps through the door of the CEO's office and my lips quirk up.

It's not even half past seven. I feel sorry for his private life, but I love his dedication to work. No wonder he made the company he started in college into the giant force it is today in only fifteen years.

Julian Sanders was a lost, hurting young man when I tried to comfort him seventeen years ago. Aged eight, I'd been mad at having to attend a funeral where I was the only child. I was bored and was exploring the Sanders' small house when I stumbled on him inside his deceased grandad's bedroom. He'd looked old to me, but now I know he must have been around twenty-three, and although I couldn't really explain the depth of the feelings his naked eyes conveyed, I'd felt like he was the saddest person in the world.

When I told Mom the name of the company I'd be working for, she'd explained it belonged to Mr. Sanders' grandson. I can't wait to meet him.

Few people had a good word to say about him during the two years he lived in Blossom Ford when he was a teenager. He'd dropped out of high school and run off to a big city and only visited his grandad on

Christmas day.

But now he was back in town as a highly respected owner of a business that generated billions in revenue and created jobs in town.

I slide out of my sneakers and slip into my favorite work heels. I switch on my laptop and once again go over the notes from Mr. Sanders' assistant, whom I was supposed to shadow for a few days. She went into early labor but left a comprehensive itemized list of instructions.

Eager to start my day and meet my new boss, I head to his office.

"Come in," a deep voice calls out in reply to my knock.

A shiver runs up my spine. I know that voice. Intimately. It whispers to me in the dark of night and sometimes when I'm showering.

I shake my head. Remind myself this is a place of work. Lothario and the delicious things he does to me don't belong here.

I square my shoulder, lift my chin and open the door.

Julian Sanders is staring at one of the laptops on his massive desk. He looks up and the greeting at the tip of my mouth vanishes.

Familiar blue eyes under thick chestnut brows root me to the spot. It's Lothario! His hair is cropped shorter at the sides and his beard is thicker, but his wide forehead and crooked nose remain the same. A dark tailored suit jacket encases his broad shoulders, just like that fateful night in New York City three years ago.

I blink, twice. Lothario is still watching me. It's hard to tell if he remembers me, but the fire in his eyes is unmistakable. It makes me feel owned, as if he branded me. Heat suffuses my whole body and face. Desire stirs my lower body. A part of my mind wonders if that look is the reason I could not forget this man.

The sound of voices, probably from the cleaning crew, brings me back to my senses.

I remind myself that I need this job. The precious pleasure this man brought me belongs only in the deepest recesses of my mind. The only thing I can do in this situation is to behave as the professional I'm supposed to be. Because Lothario is my boss, and that means nothing can ever happen between the two of us.

Once again, I set my shoulders back and lift my chin. My mouth is dry, so I clear my throat and march forward.

"Good morning Mr. sanders. It's a pleasure to meet you. I'm Winona smith, your temporary assistant." I stretch my hand out, glad I learned to fake a smile and a firm voice like a pro.

MATCHED TO PATRICK

THE O'CONNORS OF BLOSSOM FORD #1

Patrick

MINGLED LAUGHTER DRIFTS from the sitting room, bringing mixed feelings of joy and sadness. We decorated the entire house in green–it's St Patrick's Day. As usual, we've been to church and are now having beef pot roast, which Mom and Aunt Shauna insist on making every year on the feast day of St. Patrick. Dad would have been so happy to hear that laughter. Even though we gathered like today at Christmas, St Patrick's Day was his favorite holiday.

I remove more salad from the refrigerator.

"Ready for the parade of women our moms no doubt have lined up for you this year?" My cousin Lorcan asks. I know his lilting voice like I know my own.

I snap the refrigerator closed. "Will I be the only one on display?"

He winces. "You're the eldest. And you're Aunt Caitlin's only son, so you'll definitely be in the firing line. Mom will surely want to marry Riordan off first. I'll be an afterthought."

The lump in my throat prevents me from chuckling. I can't really blame Lorcan. I used to be like him. The thought of marriage drove me barmy. Not anymore.

At first I couldn't imagine myself being happy with a family, not with the crushing guilt I felt over what happened to Little Fiona. Before Dad passed, he made me promise to let go of that guilt and cherish the time I've been blessed with. Although I believed it'd never happen, little by little, I'm appreciating life.

I want what Mom and Dad had, though. They were meant for each other. Someone out there is my soulmate and the moment I find her, I'm not letting go. For the last couple of years, Mom and Aunt Shauna's matchmaking efforts haven't bothered me in the least.

I glance outside to where Riordan, my cousin and Lorcan's eldest brother, sits in the spring sun. "Riordan is not ready to get married. I doubt he'll hang around for the picnic and anyone our moms might want to set him up with."

That giant of a man is still blaming himself for what happened to his little sister Fiona, even though it's been twenty-six years since she was taken from us. Our dads were first cousins -both O'Connors. The two of us are forty-four, but I'm older than Riordan by one week. As the oldest children in the O'Connor family, it was our responsibility to make sure Fiona was safe.

Lorcan opens the back door.

"Mom is calling," he says to Rio.

It's the only thing that'll move my eldest cousin. Aunt Shauna may not be calling him now, but Riordan knows she'll soon be, wanting to make sure he spends as much time with us as possible before he scoots up the mountain.

Riordan and Lorcan's six brothers and Dad are watching TV while Mom and Aunt Shauna are chat.

"Don't forget to take good care of my friend Nara when she gets here. She was very kind to me the other day in town when I forgot my wallet," Mom reminds me.

We spend another couple of hours leisurely drinking and chatting, then get up to prepare for the outdoor picnic, which starts at four. The whole town is invited to our farm. Our parents started the tradition a few years after settling in Blossom Ford and starting a lettuce farm together, because they missed spending St Patrick's Day with their large family back in Ireland.

We put up tents on the large grass area between my house and Riordan's. Mom and Aunt Shauna used to do all the food when they were younger, but now, Lorcan gets caterers in to bring sandwiches and other finger food. By the time the townsfolk arrive, Cormac and Emmet, my youngest cousins, have set up a DJ stand which is playing upbeat music and the entire field is filled with green bunting and balloons.

I'm taking a breather from greeting people when I see a woman strolling towards Mom. Something about the way she walks catches my attention. She's wearing black skinny jeans that mold her curvy ass to perfection and a light green top that covers a pair of generous breasts and complements the sun-kissed tone of her skin. Wavy jet-black hair falls below her shoulders and shimmers in the sun.

I'm too far away to see the color of her eyes. Before I know it, I'm marching towards Mom, curiosity and something I can't name, compelling me forward.

"I'm so glad you came, Nara," Mom is saying when I reach her side on a strategic part of the field where she, Aunt Shauna, and their friend Ms. Penny can see everyone.

Tawny, that's the color of her eyes.

I answer myself as Nara greets everyone with an amiable smile that reaches her almond-shaped, yellow-brown eyes and warms the inside of my chest. She's comfortable around Mom, Aunt Shauna and their friends, even though she must be in her mid-twenties. The silver hoops on the tops of her ears glint in the sunshine.

"This is my son, Patrick." Mom points to me.

I stretch out my hand in greeting and when she holds mine; hers is small and smooth against my large and calloused one. I don't let go and she glances up at me.

That's when I know. That I've found the woman I've spent the last few years searching for.

The friendly warmth on her face is replaced by something else: interest. A tinge of pink fills her cheeks before she pulls her hand away.

Her voice cracks a little when she says hello leaving me to wonder where the confidence she exhibited a few moments ago went.

"I'll show you where the food is," I say.

"I don't want to trouble you." She looks about her. "I'll find it, thank you."

"It's no trouble at all," Mom beams at Nara. "Patrick will walk you over to the food area. Just ask him if there's anything you need to know."

A frown forms on my face as I lead the way. At my age, I'm old enough to know when a woman has the hots for me. I know Nara fancies me, but she's decided not to pursue it.

If there's one thing I'm good at, is getting to the root of a problem. Now I've found Nara, I'll have to convince her I'm the only man for her.

OTHER BOOKS BY THE AUTHOR

CURVY BRIDES OF BLOSSOM FORD SERIES

MARRYING THE PROTECTIVE PROFESSOR

MARRYING THE GRUMPY DIRECTOR

MARRYING THE POSSESSIVE NEIGHBOR

MARRYING THE WIDOWED DOCTOR

MARRYING THE SCARRED SOLDIER

MARRYING THE OBSESSIVE CEO

MARRYING THE BIG MOUNTAIN MAN

THE O'CONNORS OF BLOSSOM FORD SERIES

MATCHED TO PATRICK

ABOUT THE AUTHOR

Iris West writes short and spicy romance about alpha heroes and the women they can't help falling in love with. She loves reading all types of romance books that have a happy ending and is an avid Kdrama fan.

Follow or like her on Facebook and Goodreads.

FREE BOOK

Would you like a free book? Sign up to my mailing list at https://dl.bookfunnel.com/t191w45ryj to receive a copy of Loving My Fake Husband, a free to subscribers only, Curvy Brides of Blossom Ford Series short story.

HELP OTHERS FIND THIS BOOK

Thank you for reading Marrying The Scarred Soldier. If you enjoyed this book, please help others discover it by leaving a review at your favorite online book store.

Many thanks,

Iris xx

www.ingramcontent.com/pod-product-compliance
Lightning Source LLC
Chambersburg PA
CBHW021351160726
47994CB00007B/2911